# Amy's Light /

Written and Illustrated by Robert Nutt

DAWN PUBLICATIONS

*For you Cindy.*

Copyright © 2010 Robert Nutt

The author and publisher wish to thank the following people for their help
in presenting accurate information about fireflies: Louis Sorkin, entomologist at the
American Museum of Natural History; Marc Branham, assistant professor
at the University of Florida; and Don Salvatore, science educator
at the Museum of Science, Boston.

A Sharing Nature With Children Book

Library of Congress Cataloging-in-Publication Data
Nutt, Robert.
 Amy's light / by Robert Nutt. -- 1st ed.
   p. cm. -- (A sharing nature with children book)
 Summary: A young girl discovers a light in nature that
helps her overcome her fear of the dark. Includes an
author's note about fireflies.
 ISBN 978-1-58469-128-0 (hardback) -- ISBN 978-1-58469-129-7 (pbk.)
[1. Stories in rhyme. 2. Fireflies--Fiction. 3. Fear of the dark--Fiction.]
I. Title.
 PZ8.3.N9386Am 2010
 [E]--dc22
                                                  2009038542

Manufactured by Regent Publishing Services, Hong Kong,
Printed January, 2010, in ShenZhen, Guangdong, China
10 9 8 7 6 5 4 3 2 1
First Edition

**DAWN PUBLICATIONS**
12402 Bitney Springs Road
Nevada City, CA 95959
530-274-7775
nature@dawnpub.com

*It was a time of innocence.*

*A time of "kick the can" and climbing trees,*

*of riding bikes and skinning knees,*

*of endless days and porch swing nights,*

*watching flickering dancing lights.*

*It was a time to remember.*

It happened one night

from nowhere in sight,

by a house near the park,

when everything was dark.

In bed where she lay,

Amy wished it were day.

For the shadows on the wall

were at least twenty feet tall.

When suddenly there shone

a strange light at her feet–

from the curtains, from the window,

from the sky, from the street!

She jumped up and rushed

to the window to see

the most beautiful starlight,

dancing and free.

She smiled to herself

at the thought in her head,

then gathered her slippers

and robe by the bed.

Amy ran down the stairs

through a hall to a door,

where she reached for a jar

that she'd opened before.

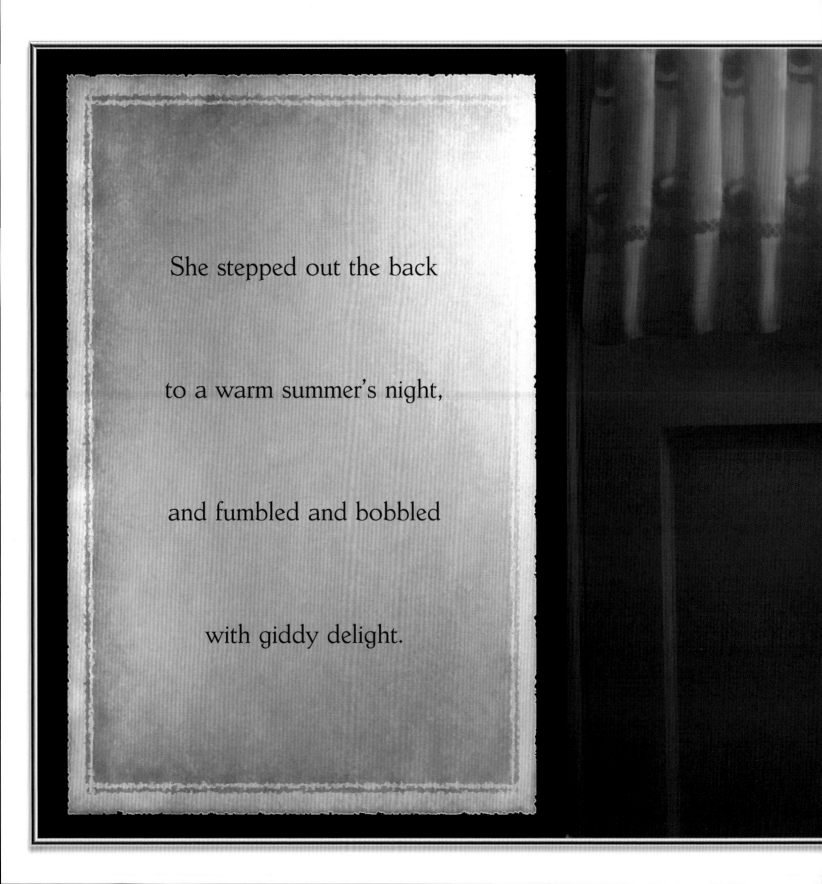

She stepped out the back

to a warm summer's night,

and fumbled and bobbled

with giddy delight.

Out in her yard

such spectacular sights ...

billions and zillions

of flickering lights!

Now she ran, then she jumped,

as she gathered with glee,

first thirteen, then sixteen,

and now twenty-three!

Amy giggled and wiggled

and held up to see,

a warm glowing jar

as bright as could be!

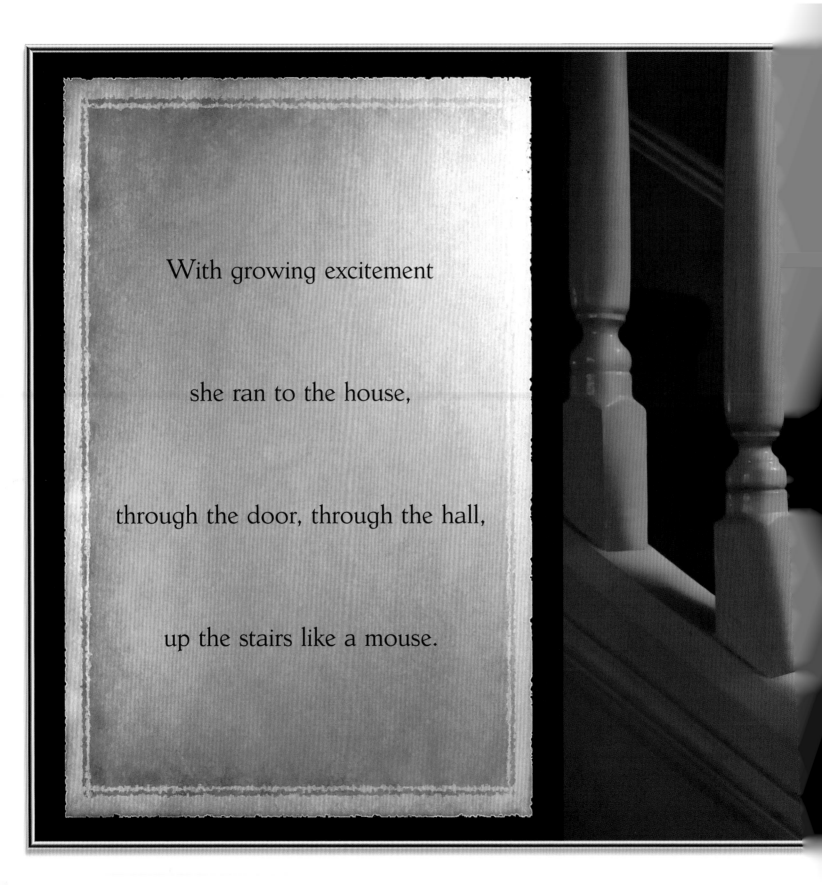

With growing excitement

she ran to the house,

through the door, through the hall,

up the stairs like a mouse.

Closing her door

she made not a sound,

for fear that her secret

would surely be found.

She took off her slippers,

dropped her robe to the floor,

to keep out the darkness

from under the door.

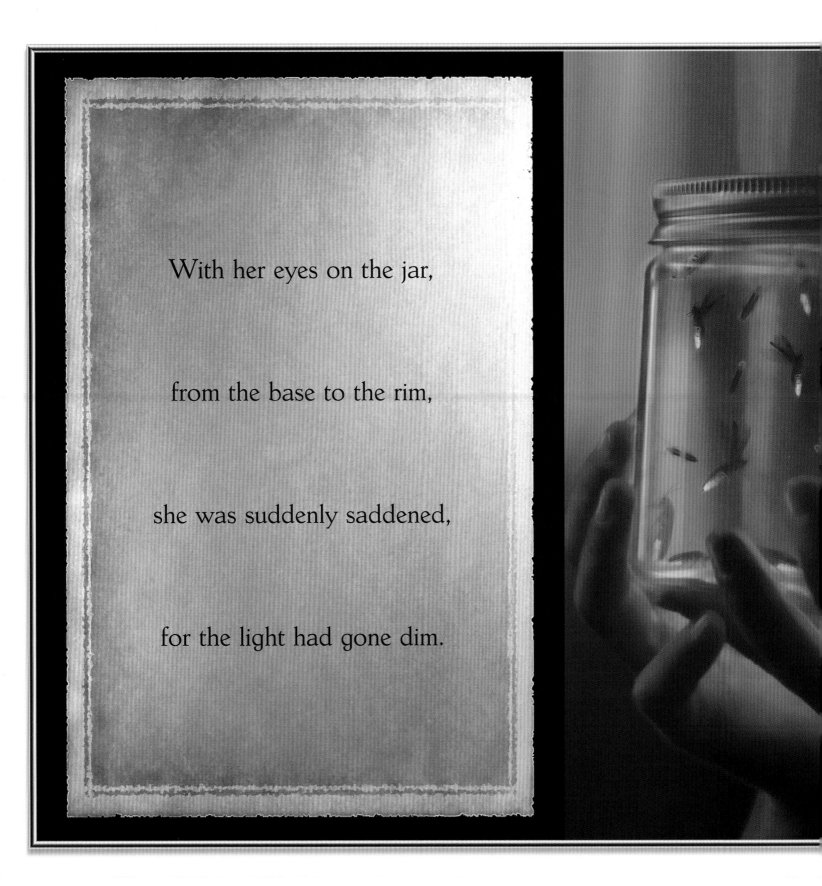

With her eyes on the jar,

from the base to the rim,

she was suddenly saddened,

for the light had gone dim.

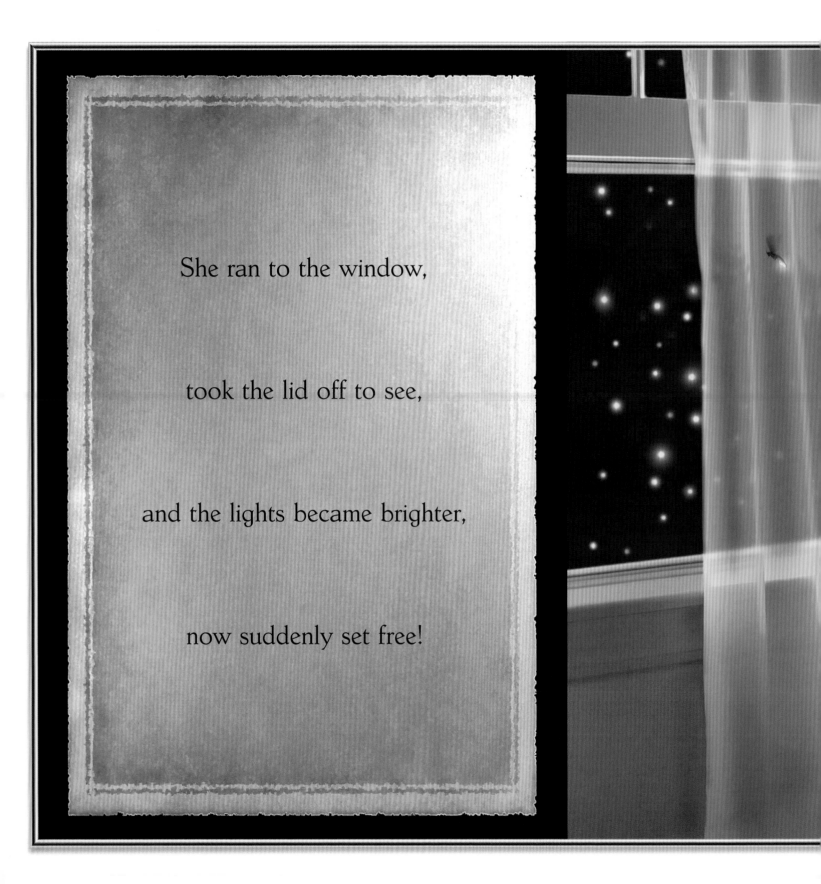

She ran to the window,

took the lid off to see,

and the lights became brighter,

now suddenly set free!

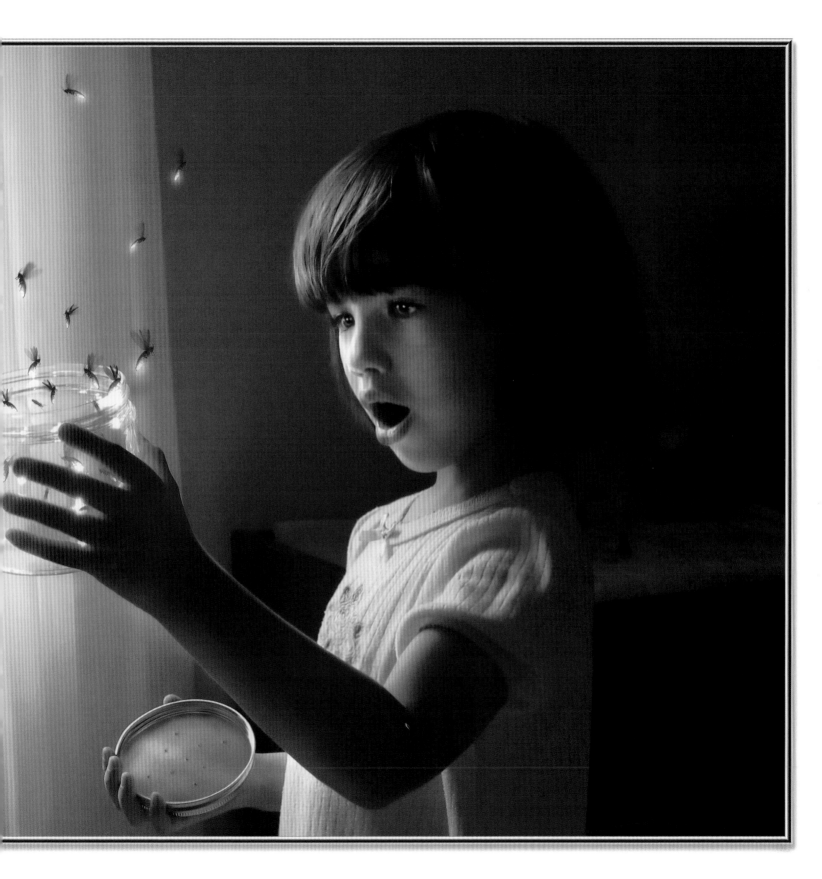

Jumping for joy,

Amy watched with delight

as they flickered and flackered

and flew out of sight.

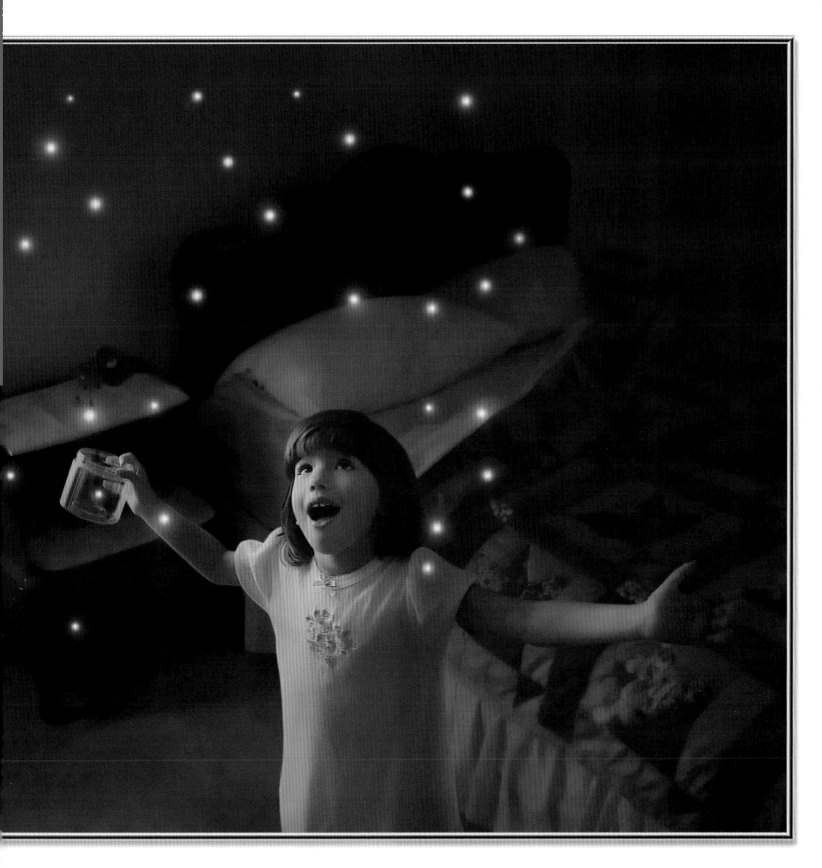

Dreamily lifting

her robe from the floor,

Amy found that her room

wasn't dark like before ...

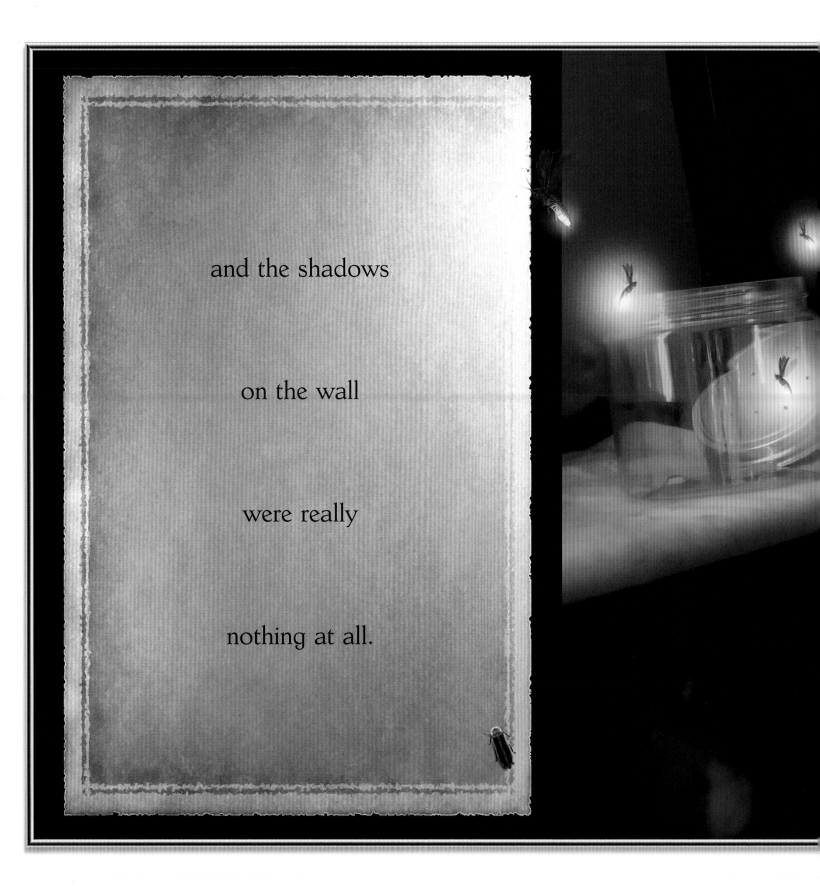

and the shadows

on the wall

were really

nothing at all.

# DID YOU KNOW?

Fireflies, often called "lightning bugs," are tiny miracles of nature. They are a kind of beetle with the innate ability to create light. Fireflies create their magical light, called *bioluminescence*, when chemicals within their abdomen interact. The result is a nearly perfect or "heatless" light. There are over 200 species of fireflies in North America and more than 2000 throughout the world. Each species has a unique style of light. This light is a key to their survival as a group.

In temperate climates, adult female fireflies lay eggs, usually in moist soil, which grow into larvae. Larvae may spend two years underground before they turn into pupae, then emerge as adult fireflies. Each adult firefly lives only a few weeks, just long enough to find a mate and lay eggs, starting the process all over again.

Male and female fireflies of the same species use their distinctive flash of light to communicate. For example, one species commonly known as the "big dipper firefly" will quickly dive just as the flash starts and lift upward to make a J-shaped flash of light. The female waiting on a shrub or in the grass recognizes the flash as a male of the same species. If she likes the look of the male's flash, she will answer with her own. Flash colors of different species range from yellow-green to amber-red.

Most observers think there are fewer fireflies now than in years past. To understand and help protect them, scientists need information. One program that helps scientists is **FIREFLY WATCH**, a program sponsored by the Museum of Science, Boston. At www.mos.org/fireflywatch you can learn to identify fireflies, report on what you find, and have your report posted along with others on an interactive map. The site also tells how to catch fireflies without harming them, and why to let them go soon. Another site, **FIREFLY FILES**, was created by Dr. Marc Branham, a leading entomologist studying fireflies. Go to http://hymfiles.biosci.ohio-state.edu/projects/FFiles/index.html for lots of firefly facts, articles, and links.